Fig
the
DREAMING PIG

Fig

the
DREAMING PIG

written by
Rebecca Roundtree

WESTBOW
PRESS®
A DIVISION OF THOMAS NELSON
& ZONDERVAN

THE HOLY BIBLE, NEW INTERNATIONAL VERSION®,
NIV® Copyright © 1973, 1978, 1984, 2011 by Biblica, Inc.®
Used by permission. All rights reserved worldwide.

Scripture taken from the New King James Version®. Copyright ©
1982 by Thomas Nelson. Used by permission. All rights reserved.

Scripture taken from the NEW AMERICAN STANDARD BIBLE®,
Copyright © 1960, 1962, 1963, 1968, 1971, 1972, 1973, 1975,
1977, 1995 by The Lockman Foundation. Used by permission.

WestBow Press books may be ordered through
booksellers or by contacting:

WestBow Press
A Division of Thomas Nelson & Zondervan
1663 Liberty Drive
Bloomington, IN 47403
www.westbowpress.com
1 (866) 928-1240

ISBN: 978-1-5127-9890-6 (sc)
ISBN: 978-1-5127-9889-0 (e)

Library of Congress Control Number: 2017912950

Print information available on the last page.

WestBow Press rev. date: 11/15/2017

Dedication

For Hannah, Haley, Hope, Tommy,
and Eliza who always make me smile!

Acknowledgments

Brett Hartdegen and Hannah Roundtree, my heart is full with much love and gratitude for your inspiration. May the devotional God wrote through us touch many as they embrace Fig's story.

Heartfelt thanks to my Mom, Bryan Roundtree, Heather Roundtree Seaman, Craig Seaman, Michelle Roundtree, Todd Sinelli, Dr. Rick Thomas, and many more family and friends who encouraged me to keep writing and pursue my dreams! Most important, thanks to God for the desire placed in my heart to reach out to children through writing!

Chapter 1

Have you ever heard of the pig who dreams of running in a race? His name is Fig, and he is eight years old. Fig lives on a farm in Woodpine Hollow with his mom, dad, and sister, Amelia. Every spring when the Annual Race of Champions comes to town, Fig wishes he was in the race. If only Fig had running shoes, then he could be in the race. But that hasn't happened yet. You see, Fig's left foot is twice as large as his other feet. No store has shoes in his size! This hasn't discouraged Fig, though. He still believes that someday he will find the perfect shoes.

One Saturday morning, Fig and his sister Amelia are outside watching their friends practice for the race. Fig is chosen to be the official referee. His favorite part is saying, *"On your marks, get set, go!"* As he kept watching everyone having fun, Fig looked at Amelia and said, "Gosh, I really wish I could be in the race, too."

"I heard there is a new shoe store opening in Hopeville this weekend. Maybe someone there can help you," Amelia suggested.

Fig's eyes brightened as he replied, "That's a great idea! I'll go there tomorrow."

The next day Fig went to Hopeville in search of new shoes. When he got there, he saw a sign for the grand opening of Cappo's Shoe Store. Balloons and streamers were everywhere! As Fig walked inside, he heard a voice say, "Welcome to Cappo's Shoe Store! What can I do for you?"

Fig turned around and saw a horse standing behind the counter. It was Cappo himself. Fig had never before seen a horse so tall. Cappo stood as high as seventeen hands put together!

"Hi, my name is Fig and I need some

running shoes. Can you help me?" he asked.

"Sure," Cappo answered. "Let's see what we can do." Cappo looked behind the counter for some tape, a pencil, a ruler, and a sheet of paper. He measured all four of Fig's feet and started drawing many different styles.

"I'm going to be in the Annual Race of Champions in two months, and I'll have to start practicing soon," Fig stated. "When do you think my shoes will be ready?" He was sure Cappo would laugh at him, but Cappo didn't laugh at all.

"That sounds very exciting," Cappo responded. "Your shoes should be ready in one week. Then you can start practicing for the big day."

Fig smiled and said, "That's great! I'll be back next week." After he told Cappo goodbye, Fig hurried home to tell his family the good news. As Fig walked out of the store he saw Conrad standing across the street. Conrad is a pig who always makes fun of Fig's foot.

All of a sudden, Fig heard Conrad shouting, "Hey everyone, look at the biggest foot in the world! Watch out or he may step on you!" Then Conrad started singing, "Fig, Fig, your foot is so big! Fig, Fig, the funny looking pig!" Fig ignored Conrad and kept walking, but that didn't stop Conrad from singing even louder! Fig began to feel embarrassed and sad. However, instead of fighting with Conrad, Fig decided to take a deep breath, count to ten, and keep walking.

Chapter 2

When Fig got back home, he told Amelia about meeting Cappo.

"I'm so happy for you," Amelia said. "That is just wonderful news!" Fig also told her about Conrad's mean song. Then his eyes filled up with tears.

"Maybe if I looked different, no one would make fun of me," Fig cried.

Amelia tried to encourage her little brother as she said, "Always remember that you are special to God. He loves everything about you and has great plans for you." Fig wiped away his tears and thanked his sister for being so nice.

Amelia happened to look at her watch and said, "Oh goodness, it's four o' clock! It's almost time for church and Mr. Tom will be speaking soon. We better go now so we're not late."

"Okay, let's go," Fig said excitedly.

Everyone always looked forward to hearing what Mr. Tom had to say. Mr. Tom is a horse who is owned by the local pastor, and he enjoys encouraging the other animals. Everyone was gathered underneath the big maple tree near the church waiting expectantly for Mr. Tom's arrival.

"Hello and welcome," Mr. Tom said as he greeted everyone. "Today I want to talk about forgiveness. Can anyone tell me what forgiveness means?" All the animals looked around at each other, but no one spoke.

"Is forgiveness when we choose not to be mad at someone anymore?" Amelia asked.

Nodding his head, Mr. Tom answered, "That's correct, Amelia." Then he asked everyone, "Have any of you ever been mad at someone who hurt your feelings?"

Fig replied, "I have."

"Me too," others said.

Looking at the crowd, Mr. Tom asked,

run faster and with more energy. Cappo made the front shoes with extra cushion since Fig walks on his tiptoes, like all pigs do.

With much excitement, Fig said, "It feels like I am walking on clouds of marshmallows!"

Fig knew that he also needed to find a coach. He figured Cappo would be the perfect one to ask since he was a former championship winner. So he decided to ask Cappo to be his coach.

"Cappo, I really need someone to help me get ready for the race," Fig said. "Would you be my coach?"

"Sure, I would be happy to be your coach," Cappo answered. "Thank you for asking."

Cappo and Fig decided to begin training early the next day. Fig was so excited he could hardly go to sleep that night! Morning came and Fig was ready for his first lesson. He arrived at Cappo's store bright and early at 7:00 a.m.

"Hello there, Fig. Are you ready for your first day of training?" Cappo asked.

"I sure am," Fig answered. "I'm going to be a great student!"

Cappo smiled and said, "I'm sure you will be." Then Cappo began explaining to Fig the importance of balancing and what to do when there are twists and turns on the race path.

"You have to be prepared for everything," Cappo instructed.

Fig humbly lowered his head and asked, "What happens if I fall down and everyone laughs at me?"

Cappo knew that Fig was concerned about tripping over his foot. "If you fall down, it's okay," Cappo said reassuringly. "All you have to do is just make sure to get back up again. A true champion knows that it doesn't matter how many times you fall. It only matters how many times you get back up."

Thinking about all the possibilities, Fig asked, "Cappo, do you think I could win the race?"

"I think you have just as much of a chance as everyone else if you practice," Cappo stated. "The most important thing to remember is to do your best and ask God to help you run the race well."

"I sure will, and if I fall down, I will make sure to get right back up!" Fig declared.

"That's the spirit!" Cappo exclaimed.

After practice, Fig rolled around in a nearby mud puddle by Cappo's store. Splashing in mud puddles helps pigs stay cool, so that's exactly what Fig did! Then Fig headed home. Fig had been walking only a few minutes when he saw Conrad running nearby. Conrad was practicing for the race, too.

"Do you really think those shoes are going to help you?" Conrad laughed. "You should just give up now. Everyone knows that I'm the fastest runner in Woodpine Hollow. Besides, if God wanted you to run in races, why did He give you such a weird foot? He probably doesn't want you to do it."

Fig looked at Conrad and boldly responded, "I think everyone who enters the race has a chance to win. You can keep making fun of me, but that will not keep me from trying. I'm going to be in the race." Then Fig continued on his way.

"I'm still going to win!" Conrad shouted.

Fig just kept walking and didn't pay any attention to Conrad. Walking along Haley Pine creek on his way home, Fig noticed Mr. Tom outside. So he decided to say Hello.

"Well, good afternoon to you," Mr. Tom said. "How are you today, Fig?"

"I'm okay," he answered. "I just finished my first day of training for the annual race."

"Good for you, Fig!" Mr. Tom said cheerfully. "I'm so proud of you!"

"Thanks, Mr. Tom," Fig replied.

Sensing that Fig had something else on his mind, Mr. Tom asked, "Is there anything else you would like to talk about?"

"Well, sort of," Fig said. "I have been praying about forgiveness and I even prayed for Conrad. I was feeling better, and then today Conrad made fun of me again. How many times am I supposed to forgive him?"

"Actually, we are never to stop forgiving others," Mr. Tom answered. "Do you think God only has a certain amount of times that He can forgive you?"

Fig humbly replied, "I guess not."

"Keep praying and God will help you forgive," Mr. Tom stated.

"Okay, I promise I'll keep praying," Fig said as he waved goodbye to Mr. Tom and then headed back home.

Over the next two months, Fig learned so much from Cappo. His confidence grew more and more everyday as he learned how to run fast, jump over rocks, and make quick turns without falling. He also learned how important it is to keep trusting God and to never give up. A few times Fig fell down and scraped his knee, but that didn't stop him. Fig got up every time. After completing Cappo's training program, Fig was so happy that his heart was overflowing with joy. Nothing was going to stop him now!

Chapter 4

At last the big day was finally here! Race day! Fig's parents, Amelia, Mr. Tom, and Cappo were all at the race to support Fig.

"We wish you all the best," Fig's Mom said as she gave him a big hug.

"Thanks, Mom. This is the neatest day ever!" Fig shouted.

"Yes, it is," she replied.

All the animals were called to get in line. Fig pinned on his race tag and was ready to go. He looked around at everyone watching and couldn't believe he was really there. His dream was coming true.

Fig looked up to the sky and said, "Thanks, God, for letting me be in the race. This is so cool!"

"Everyone on your marks," shouted a voice over the loud speaker. Fig's heart

was racing! *"Get set, go,"* said the voice, and then they were off! Fig was running well. He leaped over rocks and made quick turns without falling. He even ran through mud and didn't fall. He was so excited and having so much fun!

Fig couldn't believe he was almost in the lead! *Oh gosh, if I keep running like this, I might win! That would be awesome,* he thought. As Fig looked ahead, he saw Conrad on the ground crying. *If I stop now, there is no way I can win the race. What should I do?* he wondered. Then he remembered what Mr. Tom said about forgiving others. So Fig decided to stop and help Conrad.

"What happened to you, Conrad?" Fig asked.

"I tripped over a rock and now my foot is stuck. Go ahead and laugh. I know you want to," Conrad sighed.

"I'm not going to laugh at you. I'm here to help you," Fig replied kindly.

"But I have been so mean to you. What makes you want to help me?" Conrad asked.

"Well, I believe God wants us to forgive others and that's what I'm trying to do," Fig stated.

At that moment Conrad didn't want to make fun of Fig anymore. Conrad apologized to Fig and promised he would never make fun of him again. Then Fig moved the rock and helped Conrad stand up.

Conrad thanked Fig for helping him, and within minutes both he and Fig were back in the race. Since they were only at the halfway mark, Fig believed that he still might have a chance to win. He started to run as fast as he could to catch up with everyone else.

Before he knew it, Fig was almost in the lead again and had a wonderful thought. *Maybe I still have a chance! Maybe I could still win!* Then all of a sudden, Fig noticed that one of his shoes was starting to feel loose. Fig didn't know what else to do but keep on running.

"Please God, don't let me fall," Fig pleaded.

Just as Fig was about to make a quick turn, he tripped over a turtle and his front left shoe came off. *Bam!* Fig was face down in a deep mud puddle and so was his shoe! This was the moment Fig had feared all along. Was everyone going to laugh at him? Was he going to be able to finish the race?

With tears in his eyes, Fig looked up to the sky and said, "God, I don't understand how this could happen. I prayed not to fall and I fell anyway. Did I not say enough prayers?"

Covered in mud, Fig looked around for someone to help him. Seeing no one in sight or his shoe, Fig thought, *What am I going to do if I can't find my shoe? I can't finish the race without it.* Then Fig remembered what Cappo said about not giving up. Fig knew that God would make everything work out for good, he just didn't know how. So Fig got back up and started searching through the mud. *My shoe has to be here somewhere* thought Fig. *As soon as I find it, I'll be back on my way.*

Chapter 5

As Fig was searching for his shoe, something started to change on the inside. He wasn't thinking about winning anymore. Now he just wanted to finish the race. Fig was beginning to realize that winning isn't what is most important. It's how he runs the race that will make him a champion.

Conrad was running nearby and saw that Fig had fallen down, too. *If I help Fig, then I really won't win. Everyone expects me to win because I'm the fastest pig in town. What will everyone think if I lose?* he wondered. So Conrad pretended not to see Fig and ran on by.

The more Conrad kept running, the more he kept thinking about how Fig had just helped him. *If he wouldn't have helped*

me, I would probably still have my foot stuck under the rock. I was so mean to him and he still forgave me. Maybe God's trying to teach me a lesson too, he thought. So Conrad turned around and went to help Fig.

"Hi Fig, what happened?" Conrad asked.

Still searching for his shoe, Fig replied, "Well, I was running so fast that I tripped over a turtle. Then my shoe fell off, and now it's in the mud. I can't find it."

Thankful for what Fig did for him, Conrad said, "I'll help you."

Surprised, Fig replied, "You will? Thank you so much!"

It was taking a long time to look for Fig's shoe because the mud was so thick. By this time, Fig's other three shoes were all covered in mud, too. Minutes later Fig and Conrad heard the first place winner's name being announced. Then finally Fig found his missing shoe. It was too muddy to wear, so he knew there was no way he could run.

"I guess I will just have to walk the race with no shoes," Fig said. "Thanks for helping me, Conrad."

"You're welcome," Conrad replied.

"If you hurry, maybe you could at least come in third place," Fig suggested.

Then Conrad did something unexpected. He decided to walk the rest of the race, too. Conrad did learn a lesson that day. He learned about pride, and that it's more important to focus on others instead of himself.

Both Fig and Conrad crossed the finish line together. Fig was surprised to hear the crowd cheering his name. Everyone was so inspired that Fig never gave up.

Fig's parents, Amelia, Mr. Tom and Cappo were all shouting, "We're so proud of you!"

Everyone was so happy for him. Fig walked up to his family and friends and gave everyone a great big hug. Then his name was called to go to the winner's circle. So Fig walked over to see Mr. Andrew, the race chairman.

"Fig, you have shown us all how to be a true champion," Mr. Andrew said. "You never gave up. Please accept this ribbon in honor of your perseverance to finish the race."

Fig was so excited! No one was laughing at him anymore. Enjoying the moment, he just kept looking at his shiny new ribbon and smiling.

"We also want to invite you to come along with us this summer as we travel across the country to other races. Would you like to join us?" Mr. Andrew asked.

Fig shouted, "Of course, I'll go! That's awesome!" Fig's heart was filled with joy as he thanked God for making his dream come true.

As he was enjoying the celebration, Fig realized that now he wants to start teaching other animals about running, and most importantly, he wants to speak about the power of forgiveness and trusting God always. He also plans to keep asking others his favorite question, "What is your dream?"

So, the next time you're wondering about reaching for your dreams, always think of Fig and how he never gave up!

Fig the Dreaming Pig
Devotional

Day 1: Self-Esteem

In Chapter 1 we read about Fig and his dream of running in the Annual Race of Champions. After his sister Amelia told him about the new shoe store across town, Fig set out on the brave journey to search for shoes that would fit his over-sized left foot. He was so excited the next day about meeting Cappo, the shoe store owner. Then he saw Conrad near the store who was laughing and singing a mean song about him. Even though this embarrassed Fig and hurt his feelings, he decided not to fight and kept walking on by.

Have you ever had someone make fun of you? If yes, how did that make you feel? Be encouraged that God loves you. You are special in His eyes! Write your answers in the space below and share with a loved one.

_____

_____

_____

_____

_____

_____

_____

_____

_____

"I will give thanks to You, for I am fearfully and wonderfully made;
Wonderful are Your works, And my soul knows it very well."
(Psalm 139:14 NIV)

Day 1 Prayer:

Dear Lord, thank You for creating me. Please help me to remember that I am special in Your eyes and that You love me. If someone makes fun of me and hurts my feelings, please help my heart to forgive and pray for them. Please help me to keep trusting in You and to never forget that I am made in Your image. Amen.

Day 2: Courage, Fear and Faith

In Chapter 2 we read about Fig telling Amelia what happened on his journey to the store. Fig began to wonder if others would stop making fun of him if he looked different. He was starting to become afraid of being in the race. Then his sister invited Fig to church to hear Mr. Tom's sermon. Being around family and friends learning about God made Fig feel much better. Fig showed great courage by sharing his thoughts and going to church even though his feelings were hurt.

Has there ever been a time when you wanted to try something new but you were afraid? For example, maybe you're thinking about trying out for a baseball team, a soccer team or cheerleading but haven't done so yet. Are you afraid others will make fun of you for trying? Always remember that it is okay to be a little nervous about trying something new. God will give you courage to do what He wants with the gifts and talents He has placed inside you.

List 4 positive statements about yourself!

1.

2.

3.

4.

"I can do all things through Christ who strengthens me."
(Phillippians 4:13 NKJV)

"Therefore I tell you, whatever you ask for in prayer, believe that you have received it, and it will be yours."
(Mark 11:24 NIV)

Day 2 Prayer:

Dear Lord, thank You for giving me courage. The next time I feel afraid, please help me remember that You will never leave me and that You will give me faith to face any fear. Thank You for loving me whenever I may get afraid. I believe You have given me special gifts and talents that were made just for me to share for Your purpose. Please help me honor You in all I do. Amen.

Day 3: Forgiveness and Perseverance

In Chapter 3 we read about Fig getting his brand new shoes. This was a very exciting time! Fig enjoyed training for the race with Cappo. Fig had also been praying for Conrad. But Fig's feelings got hurt when Conrad made fun of him again. Fig didn't understand why God would allow Conrad to be mean even when Fig was trying to forgive.

On Fig's way home from practice, Mr. Tom reminded Fig of the importance of forgiveness and never giving up. God does not have a certain amount of times that He will forgive us. That means we also don't have a certain amount of times we can forgive others. Forgiveness is not always easy and we need God's help. Mr. Tom encouraged Fig to keep praying and to ask God for help. God taught Fig's heart how to keep forgiving. God also gave Fig the strength and perseverance to keep training for the race. Always remember that God loves you more than anything and you have a special purpose.

What does forgiveness mean to you? Is there someone in your life you need to forgive? Write your answers in the space below and share with a loved one.

_____
_____
_____
_____
_____
_____
_____

"Be kind to one another, tender-hearted, forgiving each other, just as God in Christ also has forgiven you."
(Ephesians 4:32 NASB)

Day 3 Prayer:

Dear Lord, thank You for loving me. Please help me to forgive _____ for being unkind. I pray that their heart will not be mad anymore. I also pray they will know how much You love them. Please help me to ask others for forgiveness too, when I do something wrong. Amen.

Day 4: Prayer

In Chapter 4 we read about the big race day. Fig was so excited! He even thought he might win. But when Conrad's foot got stuck under a rock, Fig stopped running. He showed much kindness and forgiveness by helping Conrad. Then later, Fig tripped. His heart was broken as he searched for his shoe in the mud. He didn't understand why his prayers weren't answered about not falling. But Fig knew God would make everything work out for good.

Have you ever prayed about something and things didn't turn out the way you hoped? Maybe you prayed to be selected for a team and that didn't happen. Or, maybe you are praying for someone to feel better and they are still sick. Be encouraged that God always hears our prayers when we pray with a pure heart. God wants us to know that He is ready to listen. He even tells us in Jeremiah 33:3 to "Call to Me and I will answer you and tell you great and unsearchable things you do not know."

When we give our prayers to God, we can trust that He will answer. We never have to worry about our prayers not being "good enough". We only need to keep talking to God and asking Him to speak to our heart. His answers are either yes, no or not right now. Be encouraged that God knows what is best. Keep trusting Him.

List your prayer requests. Ask a loved one to pray with you.

1.

2.

3.

4.

"And we know that in all things God works for the good of those who love Him, who have been called according to His purpose."
(Romans 8:28 NIV)

Day 4 Prayer:

Dear Lord, thank You for loving me and always listening to my prayers. Please help me to wait patiently for Your answers. Please help me to trust You even when my prayers are answered in ways that I don't understand. Amen.

Day 5: Run your race

In Chapter 5 we read about Fig's heart learning that winning isn't what matters the most. Conrad was not nice when he ran by Fig and didn't stop to help him. Conrad began to realize that if Fig had not helped him, maybe his foot would still be stuck under the rock. God began to soften Conrad's heart. Conrad showed much kindness by deciding to help Fig and walk across the finish line with him.

Fig's dream came true of being in the race. Now he wants to tell others about the power of forgiveness, never giving up and believing in the dreams God gave them. Have you ever encouraged anyone by your actions or through sharing kind words? Has anyone ever encouraged you? Write your answers in the space below and share with a loved one.

_____

_____

_____

_____

_____

_____

_____

*Remember, never give up. With God, all things are possible! What is your dream?

_____

_____

_____

_____

"I have fought the good fight, I have finished the race, I have kept the faith."
(2Timothy 4:7 NIV)

Day 5 Prayer:

Dear Lord, thank You for helping me to show kindness through my actions and words. Thank You for helping me believe in my dreams. Please help me to encourage others to never give up and to always show kindness and forgiveness toward others. I pray they will always believe in their dreams. I pray that my light inside will always shine as I tell others how much You love them, too. Amen.

Scripture Memory Verses

"Call to Me and I will answer you and tell you great and unsearchable things you do not know.
(Jeremiah 33:3 NIV)

"I will give thanks to You, for I am fearfully and wonderfully made; Wonderful are Your works, And my soul knows it very well."
(Psalm 139.14 NASB)

"I can do all things through Christ who strengthens me."
(Phillippians 4:13 NKJV)

"Therefore I tell you, whatever you ask for in prayer, believe that you have received it, and it will be yours."
(Mark 11:24 NIV)

"Be kind to one another, tender-hearted, forgiving each other, just as God in Christ also has forgiven you."
(Ephesians 4:32 NASB)

"And we know that in all things God works for the good of those who love Him, who have been called according to His purpose."
(Romans 8:28 NIV)

"I have fought the good fight, I have finished the race, I have kept the faith."
(2 Timothy 4:7 NIV)

Printed in the United States
By Bookmasters